HEARTBOUND SOULS

COASTAL CUPID
BOOK 1

JAX WILDER

RAINBOW QUARTZ PUBLISHING

Edmonds WA, 98026 First Edition: 2024

Cover design by Miranda Townsend — Interior design by Miranda Townsend

Tarot Card description by Lorelai Hamilton from the book Teenage Tarot – used with permission.

Library of Congress Cataloging-in-Publication Data has been applied for.

For permissions or inquiries, please contact: Rainbow Quartz Publishing rainbowquartzpublishing@gmail.com RQPublishing.com

For Emma Caulfield who inspired this whole series

PROLOGUE

Welcome to Coral Cove's Coastal Cupid
Eternal Flame Kindlers Since 1985

Nestled in the heart of Coral Cove—a seaside town where the sun kisses the ocean and magic dances on every breeze —there's a little office that has been setting hearts aflame for nearly four decades.

This is *Coastal Cupid,* a place where love isn't just a possibility.

It's a promise.

Here, it doesn't matter if you're a love-struck human, a brooding vampire, or a mischievous fae with a flair for trouble. Everyone who walks through our doors shares one thing in common — a desire to find the soul they were destined for, the one who will set their heart blazing brighter than the stars.

Coral Cove itself isn't your average beachside getaway.

On the surface, it looks like any charming coastal town, with sun-bleached boardwalks, bustling cafés, and locals who all seem to know one another by name. But beneath the quaint façades lies something far more extraordinary.

This town sits at a crossroads where three realms meet: the human world, the shadow world, and the fae world. Here, the veil between dimensions is as thin as a whisper. Spells drift through the ocean mist like perfume. Fae bargains are struck over steaming cups of espresso. And on certain nights, when the moonlight hits the waves just right, you might glimpse creatures no mortal storybook could ever fully capture.

In this extraordinary vortex of magic and mystery, finding love isn't just difficult—it's *complicated*.

Different species, conflicting magic, ancient rivalries… it's enough to make even the most star-crossed lovers think twice.

That's where Coastal Cupid comes in.

. . .

AT COASTAL CUPID, WE DON'T JUST MATCH YOU WITH someone "compatible."

We find your Heartbound Soul—the one person destined to set your heart aflame, no matter if it beats in rhythm with the moon, the tide, or the stars.

Our secret weapon? A little piece of enchanted technology known as the SoulSync Implant.

The SoulSync was designed with one purpose — to cut through the noise and guide you straight to your other half.

A small, discreet implant rests just beneath the skin of your wrist, blending seamlessly with your body's natural energy. Once activated, it connects to your unique bio-signature—a unique blend of your DNA, emotional patterns, and intrinsic magical frequency.

Unlike old-fashioned matching spells, the Soul-Sync doesn't require both partners to have one. It works independently, constantly scanning for resonance between your unique imprint and that of your potential soulmates.

Imagine for a moment.

You're walking through the streets of Coral Cove when, suddenly, a warm rush floods your wrist, a faint golden glow beneath the skin. Or maybe a single word appears in your mind like a whisper, or a memory you've never lived floods your senses as you lock eyes with a stranger.

That's the SoulSync at work—subtle, powerful, and deeply personal.

Best of all, it's customizable.

Prefer a soft auditory chime when your soulmate is near? Done.

Want to see a flash of imagery, like a fleeting vision of a shared future? Easily arranged.

Some clients even choose a physical cue, like a delicate pulse or a fluttering warmth that spreads across the skin.

Every SoulSync experience is as unique as the soul it's bound to find.

The SoulSync's creation was nothing short of revolutionary, but the heart behind it was even more magical.

Nearly forty years ago, Valarie Cupid, the enigmatic founder of Coastal Cupid, opened the office with a single mission: to kindle eternal flames in the hearts of the extraordinary.

Valarie is a figure of mystery in Coral Cove. She rarely leaves the shop, but locals whisper about the shimmering mark on her wrist and the way her gaze seems to pierce straight into your soul. Some say she invented the SoulSync with magic so old it predates even the fae. Others believe she herself is a love spirit, sent to ensure no soul goes unclaimed.

Whatever the truth, her success is undeniable.

Coastal Cupid has a perfect track record.

Every match she's made has endured—sometimes in this lifetime, sometimes across many.

No love is too strange or too impossible for us to find.

From werewolves to mermaids, demons to angels, zombies to aliens, we've seen it all—and matched them all, too. No species, no identity, no desire is too unique for love to find its way.

Because in Coral Cove, magic doesn't just fill the air.

It fills the heart.

So, if you're ready to dive into a world where love transcends every boundary, come find us. Your Heartbound Soul is out there, waiting for you.

And here at Coastal Cupid, we don't just believe in happily ever after.

We *create* it.

CHAPTER 1
CLARK

T he night breathed around me as I stepped onto Water Street, carrying the mingled scents of brine, sugar, and something faintly metallic that always seemed to linger near the docks. The air was damp and cool, clinging to my skin like mist. Somewhere out on the water, a foghorn let out a low, mournful wail that seemed to vibrate in my bones.

Most people would describe Coral Cove as charming.

Quaint.

Safe.

But walking its streets at night, when the tourists had retreated to their seaside rentals and the shops had shuttered their windows, you could sense something else beneath the picturesque surface. The cobblestone sidewalks were slick with condensation, their uneven stones older than the town's recorded history. Street-lamps cast pools of golden light that didn't quite reach the shadows, leaving pockets of darkness that felt almost… watchful.

It was the only time I was free to wander.

The day belonged to everyone else—to sunbathers sprawled on towels, kids chasing gulls along the shoreline, couples licking ice cream from each other's fingers while the salt wind tangled their hair. I'd watched them from behind drawn curtains, safe in the shadows, my skin protected by layers of glass and heavy blinds.

Daylight was my enemy.

My condition, xeroderma pigmentosum—or XP—made the sun's rays as deadly as fire. Even a brief exposure could burn, blister, or worse. For me, a walk under the noon sky wasn't just dangerous; it was unthinkable. While others lived in the rhythm of sunrise and sunset, I existed in the narrow hours between dusk and dawn, a phantom haunting the edges of their world.

Some nights, like tonight, that reality felt suffocating.

Other nights, it felt like freedom.

I slipped my hands into the pockets of my hoodie and breathed deeply, inhaling the night. It smelled of fried food from the boardwalk, damp sand, and the lingering sweetness of the bakery two blocks over, where they baked cinnamon rolls for the morning rush.

My stomach growled loudly enough to make me laugh. "Okay, okay. Waterfront Pizza it is."

The promise of melted cheese and their famous Margherita carried me forward. My sneakers scuffed softly against the cobblestones as I passed shuttered gift shops and darkened cafés. A few of the late-night businesses were still glowing, their windows fogged with warmth and laughter. I envied the people inside those places—their ease, their belonging.

By the time I reached the pizzeria, the ache in my stomach had sharpened to a pang. I pushed open the weathered wooden door, and the little bell above it jingled merrily.

The warmth hit me first, followed by the glorious aroma of baked dough and fresh basil. It wrapped around me like a blanket, momentarily pushing back the chill I'd carried in from the street. The restaurant was cozy, with mismatched chairs, scuffed tables, and walls covered in framed photographs of fishermen holding up their prize catches.

"Clark?"

The familiar voice made me pause mid-step. I turned and scanned the booths until my gaze landed on Sabrina, waving from the far corner. Her wavy auburn hair caught the light like polished copper, and she was grinning so wide it was a wonder her cheeks didn't hurt.

I broke into a smile of my own. "Sabrina! No freaking way."

We collided in a hug that smelled like vanilla lotion and some floral perfume I couldn't place. Her laugh bubbled against my shoulder before she pulled back to look me over.

"Girl, you look amazing," she said, hands on my arms like she couldn't quite believe I was real. "It's been, what, three years? Four?"

"Three and a half," I said automatically, because of course I'd kept count. "And you look exactly the same. Like you've been drinking youth potions or something."

She wiggled her brows. "Well, you never know. Magic is real here, after all."

The joke landed a little too close to the truth, and for a heartbeat, neither of us laughed.

Then she brightened, motioning toward the booth. "Sit, sit! I was just about to order dessert."

I slid into the seat across from her, the cracked vinyl sticking slightly to the back of my legs. "I was actually just stopping in for a slice to-go, but… wow, it's really good to see you. Where have you been hiding?"

Her question was innocent enough, but it struck something tender in me. Where had I been hiding? Inside, mostly. In the safe darkness of my apartment, away from daylight and crowds and the temptation to want what I couldn't have.

"You know me," I said lightly, "always lurking like a vampire."

Sabrina's smile faltered. Guilt flickered across her face, as if she regretted bringing up my XP at all.

I waved a hand. "It's fine. Really. The sun's still trying to murder me every day. No change there."

That broke the tension, and she laughed, though her eyes stayed soft with concern.

We caught up for a few minutes—her new job, my boring routines—before she leaned forward with a mischievous glint in her gaze.

"So…" she said, drawing out the word. "How's your love life?"

I nearly snorted water through my nose. "Nonexistent. Do you even have to ask?"

Her grin widened. "I don't believe that for a

second. You've got that *look*. Like someone's been haunting your dreams."

"Well, I wouldn't say there's anyone special," I began slowly, "but I did have a... let's call it an *experience* at the Arcane Room not too long ago."

The memory rose unbidden, vivid and sharp, stealing my breath as if I were standing there again.

There had been a moment when I opened my eyes and forgot I had XP.

For one glorious, impossible second, I was *normal*.

The sun blazed above me, golden and unrelenting. Panic hit me first—pure instinct. My arms flew up to shield my face, my body bracing for the inevitable pain. All my life, I'd been told the sun would destroy me, blister my skin, burn me alive in minutes.

But there was no searing pain.

No death.

Only warmth.

Tentatively, I lowered my arms. The beach stretched endlessly before me, white sand glittering like powdered gold, waves lapping gently at the shore. The air was salted and sweet, filled with the cries of distant gulls and the rhythmic whisper of the ocean.

I stood in the sunlight, whole and unharmed.

"This isn't real," I breathed, my heart pounding.

A voice answered, smooth and steady, coming from the surf itself. "It's real *enough*."

I spun around.

He emerged from the waves like some untamed god of the sea, water sliding over dark, sun-kissed skin, his black hair plastered to his brow. His smile was wicked and devastating, like he knew every secret I'd never spoken aloud.

"You're safe here," he said simply, his gaze holding mine. "This world was made for you."

"Who are you?" My voice trembled, fear and awe tangled together.

"Kade." His name wrapped around me like a promise. "And you, Clark, are finally free."

The word *free* cracked something inside me.

For the first time in my life, I stepped forward into the sunlight instead of away from it. The sand was warm beneath my bare feet, the sun's caress sinking into my bones. Tears stung my eyes, though they didn't burn.

"I shouldn't be able to do this," I whispered. "This should kill me."

"Not here," Kade murmured. He reached out, his fingers brushing mine. His touch was warm, grounding, *real*. "Here, you get to have everything you've ever been denied."

The world shimmered with possibility, the edges of it bending to my unspoken desires. I wanted to laugh, to run, to claim this dream as my own. But more than anything, I wanted *him*.

I reached for Kade and kissed him, fiercely, desperately. He tasted like salt and heat and freedom. His arms came around me, strong and certain, pulling me flush against him. My body, so long confined by fear and shadows, came alive under his hands.

We sank to the warm sand, tangled together. The sunlight washed over me, over *us*, gilding every kiss, every sigh.

For once, I wasn't the girl defined by her illness.

I wasn't the fragile one who couldn't risk daylight.

Here, I was a woman who could take what she wanted.

And what I wanted was *him*.

When Kade whispered my name against my skin, it felt like a vow. A claiming. A promise that this dream was more than just a fleeting fantasy—that it meant something neither of us could deny.

. . .

"CLARK?" SABRINA'S VOICE SNAPPED ME BACK TO the present. I blinked, the cozy pizza parlor swimming into focus. She was watching me, curiosity and concern mingling on her face.

"You okay? You kind of zoned out there."

I forced a shaky laugh, rubbing the back of my neck. "Yeah, sorry. Just… remembering." My cheeks burned. "It wasn't *real* real. Just… a dream. But it felt like it was."

Even as I said it, I felt the faintest warmth on my wrist, a phantom echo that hadn't been there before.

Almost like Kade was out there, listening.

We left Waterfront Pizza behind, stepping into the cool mist of the night. The streets were quieter now, the fog creeping low along the cobblestones like a living thing, curling around streetlamps and storefronts. A few neon signs buzzed faintly, their colors muted through the haze.

Sabrina walked beside me, practically buzzing with excitement, her auburn hair catching the glow of the lights. "I can't believe I get to be the one to bring you here for the first time," she said, practically bouncing on her toes. "Coastal Cupid changes lives, Clark. It *changed mine.*"

"Changed yours?" I raised a brow, tugging my hoodie tighter against the damp air. "Why do I get the feeling there's a whole story there you're not telling me?"

Sabrina grinned, her teeth flashing white in the dim light. "Oh, there is. But tonight's about *you*, not me. Let's just say Valarie Cupid has this way of... seeing people. She doesn't just match you with some- one. She matches you with the *right* someone."

Her words sent a little flutter through my chest, though I tried to ignore it.

We rounded a corner, and there it was.

The Coastal Cupid building stood at the end of a narrow lane, its heart-shaped windows glowing softly pink in the fog. Above the door hung a sign that made me pause—a stylized skeleton clutching a heart. The bones were painted in gleaming white enamel, and the heart it held glowed faintly, pulsing like it was alive.

I stopped dead in my tracks. "Uh, Sab... why is there a skeleton on your magical matchmaking business?"

She giggled, linking her arm through mine and pulling me forward. "It's a little inside joke. The idea is that when you've found your *Heartbound Soul*, your love lasts until you're both skeletons—forever and ever, till death and beyond."

"That's... surprisingly morbid for a dating

service," I said, though a reluctant smile tugged at my lips.

"Morbid but kind of romantic, right?" she teased, giving me a nudge.

Inside, the space was bubbly chaos in the best possible way.

The front lobby looked like a mix between a boutique spa and a candy store designed by a love-struck fae. Plush white furniture with heart-shaped backs, glowing pink lanterns that hovered a few inches off the floor, and walls lined with framed success stories—photographs of couples kissing on beaches, dancing under starry skies, holding hands across realms.

The air smelled like warm sugar and citrus, like someone had bottled up joy and sprayed it into every corner.

I blinked, taking it all in. "Okay, wow. This is... a lot."

"Wait until you meet Valarie," Sabrina said, practically skipping ahead of me. "She's *extra* in the best way."

As we crossed the room, I noticed the little magical touches everywhere: clipboards floated lazily through the air, pages fluttering like wings. A tiny pixie in a sparkly pink dress zipped past, giggling and dropping glitter as she carried a stack of intake forms twice her size. A heart-shaped clock on the far wall ticked loudly—and then, to my shock, it actually *beat*, like a real, living heart.

"Please tell me that clock isn't alive," I muttered.

Sabrina just smirked. "Everything here is alive, in its own way. Magic likes to... meddle."

Sabrina guided me to a sleek white desk tucked in the back corner. The surface was pristine, glowing faintly as though lit from within. A floating quill dipped itself into an inkpot and started scribbling the moment we sat down.

"Let's start with your intake form," she said, her tone all business now. "We need to get a full picture of who you are so Valarie can get the clearest read possible."

I groaned but took the offered parchment, filling out questions about my life, dreams, and—most painfully—my romantic history.

The questions were surprisingly personal.

What do you fear most in a relationship?

What do you wish someone would see in you that no one ever has?

What would you give up to be truly loved?

By the time I finished, my hands were trembling. "This feels like therapy with glitter."

Sabrina chuckled. "Pretty much. Only with a way better outcome."

When I handed the form back, the quill lifted it into the air and whisked it away toward a glowing chute in the wall. The paper vanished with a soft *pop*, leaving behind the faint scent of rose petals.

Sabrina's expression turned serious, though her eyes still sparkled with excitement.

"Okay, this is the big part, Clark. The thing that sets Coastal Cupid apart from literally *every other* matchmaking service in existence."

She opened a velvet-lined box, revealing a small silver device shaped like a teardrop. It gleamed softly, almost alive, like it was breathing in time with my pulse.

"This," she said reverently, "is the SoulSync Implant. It's permanent, discreet, and completely painless to install. Once it's bonded to you, it connects to your unique bio-signature—a magical blend of your DNA, emotional patterns, and intrinsic energy."

I frowned, fascinated despite myself. "And this… what? Pings when my soulmate walks by?"

Her grin widened. "Exactly. It doesn't need the other person to have one—it's completely independent. When you're near your true match, the Soul-

Sync activates in whatever way you choose. A warmth in your wrist, a soft chime, even a vivid flash of memory."

"Memory?" My voice cracked slightly.

"Yep. Some people see glimpses of shared moments they haven't lived yet." She gave a little shrug. "Love is weird like that."

I swallowed, my thoughts immediately darting to Kade. To that night in the Arcane Room and the way it had felt like we'd already known each other forever.

Sabrina leaned closer, her tone softening. "I know this feels scary. But think about it, Clark—your whole life, you've been isolated. You've had to keep the world at arm's length because of your condition. This is your chance to finally *find* someone who won't just tolerate that—they'll understand it, even cherish it."

My throat tightened. "And if they don't exist?"

Sabrina smiled, radiant and certain. "They do. Valarie's never wrong. When you meet your Heartbound Soul, you'll *know*."

I hesitated for a long moment, my pulse thudding in my ears. Then, slowly, I extended my wrist.

"Okay," I whispered. "Do it."

Sabrina counted softly, "One, two, three—" and pressed the device against my skin.

There was a sharp pinch, like the sting of a needle, and then—heat. Not burning, but a warm, spreading glow that moved through my veins like liquid sunlight. My breath caught as images flared behind my eyes: a hand brushing my cheek, a deep laugh that wasn't mine, the crash of ocean waves beneath a sky filled with stars.

And then, just as quickly, it was gone.

I gasped, clutching my wrist. A delicate heart-shaped mark now shimmered faintly on my skin, glowing before fading to a soft pink outline.

"What… what was that?" My voice shook.

"The moment your SoulSync bonded to you," Sabrina said gently. "It's officially attuned. Now, whenever your true match is near, you'll feel it."

I traced the tiny heart with my fingertip, a strange cocktail of fear and hope swirling in my chest.

"It almost felt like…" I trailed off, unsure how to explain it.

"Like destiny?" Sabrina offered, her smile knowing.

I nodded slowly. "Yeah. Exactly like that."

As we left Coastal Cupid, the cool night air felt sharper, almost too real after the magic of the office. The heart mark on my wrist tingled faintly beneath my sleeve, a reminder that my life had just shifted in a way I couldn't take back.

Friday.

That was when I'd meet Valarie Cupid herself.

And maybe—just maybe—take the first step toward finding the one person who might finally understand me.

I shoved my hands into my pockets and walked beside Sabrina in silence, my thoughts looping back to a pair of gray storm-cloud eyes and a memory of warmth that wasn't just a dream.

Because what if... what if my soulmate wasn't a stranger at all?

CHAPTER 2
KADE

The bar in Middletown wore its neon like war paint—bleeding reds and blues over polished chrome, arcade cabinets chiming in a chorus that never quite landed on the same note twice. The room smelled of beer foam and sea-salt air that drifted in each time the door swung open, carrying a faint tang of ozone that told me the veil was thinner here tonight than it should've been.

I don't usually haunt places like this. Too bright. Too loud. Too many mirrors to catch a reflection that isn't mine.

But I'd chosen this face for a reason—short dark hair, clean jaw, shoulders broad enough to turn a head without turning suspicion. Human enough. Harmless enough. The glamour fit, but it was still a cage. A skin one size too tight, the edges of me pressing against it, asking to be let out.

I told myself I'd come for anonymity. For noise loud enough to drown thought.

The truth was simpler.

I'd come because I couldn't stop thinking about her.

I leaned on the bar and let the rhythm of the place move through me—the clack of ice in glasses, a pinball bell trilling, the rising cheer around a darts bullseye—until something shifted under the din. A pulse. Not sound, not light. Resonance.

I felt her before I saw her.

Clark stood at the Cyclone machine, the cabinet lights flickering amber across copper-red curls. She was all focus and precision, hips angled, wrists loose, eyes narrowed as she coaxed the ball up the ramp and into a bonus that sent the scoreboard exploding with points. The neon made a halo of her hair; the set of her mouth said she didn't need one.

The sight of her hit like undertow. In my mind she was sunlight—laughing on a dream-beach, the taste of salt on her tongue, the way she'd said mine and meant it. Here, the light was harsher, but she wore it the same way, like a dare.

A pair of guys at the next cabinet watched her

unabashedly. Jealousy flared, quick and stupid. I swallowed it, finished my drink, and set the glass down so gently it didn't make a sound.

If I hesitated, I'd talk myself out of it. If I moved, I'd risk everything I'd kept contained.

I moved.

I picked my moment the way you pick a lock—slow, precise, certain. I drifted to her side just as the ball rattled inside a wireform and teetered for a breath at the lip.

"You know," I said, leaning a shoulder against the machine, "they say Cyclone's all about timing. Lucky for you, timing happens to be my specialty."

She twitched, attention splintering. The ball slipped past the flippers and vanished with a cruel little *chirp*.

Her head snapped toward me, eyes flashing. "Seriously? You just cost me my best score of the night."

Her anger was a blade; it slid right beneath my ribs and lodged somewhere warm. I couldn't help the smile. "Guess that means I owe you a drink."

She looked me over—slow, assessing. The corners of her mouth ticked up. "At the very least."

"Name it."

"Whiskey. Neat." Smooth voice. Smoother spine.

At the bar, the bartender slid two tumblers across the lacquer. When I handed Clark's over to her, our fingers brushed. The contact crackled—more than static, more than chance. Something at her wrist purred against my palm, an almost-imperceptible thrum, as if a hidden charm had woken and said, *Ah. There you are.*

Her eyes widened, just for a beat, before she hid it behind a sip. I hid nothing; I wanted her to see the way she rattled me.

"So," I said lightly, "what's your game of choice?"

"Depends on the night." Her brow arched. "Let me guess—you're about to challenge me to one, aren't you?"

"Medieval Madness," I said, letting the words fall like a coin into a well. "It's a classic."

She laughed, warm and rich. "I'm not playing whatever you've mastered just so you can show off and crush me."

"I'd never dream of crushing you." Not when the only thing I wanted to do was fall at her feet. I fished a quarter from my pocket and let it dance over my knuckles. "How about a compromise? Heads, we play Medieval. Tails, we stay with Cyclone."

Suspicion sharpened her smile. "And if it lands on heads, how do I know you didn't cheat?"

"You'll just have to trust me." I flicked the coin high. It spun into the neon haze, caught the red of a beer sign, the blue of a jukebox, and came down to kiss the back of my hand. Heads.

She narrowed her eyes. "Double-headed?"

I placed the coin in her palm. My glamour flexed —a breath, no more—nudging reality back into the shape she expected. By the time she turned it over, it was perfectly ordinary.

"Fine," she said, rolling her eyes, handing it back. "Let's play your game."

We slid into position at Medieval Madness, shoulders brushing, the machine's LEDs painting our hands in jewel tones. From the first launch, the air between us tightened to a humming wire. I watched her aim, the way tension gathered in her forearms right before she struck.

"You've got excellent control," I murmured, close enough for her to catch cedar and sea on my skin. "But you lock your elbows at the last second. Breathe. Let the ball come to you."

She didn't look over. "You're distracting me on purpose."

"Is it working?"

Her mouth betrayed her with a small, reluctant smile. "Maybe."

We traded shots and quips. She bumped the cabinet with a smart, precise hip-check to save a drain; I clucked my tongue. "Naughty."

"Says the man who cheated at a coin toss." She nudged me back, just enough to spark heat where we connected.

I wanted to tell her the truth. That I knew the taste of her laugh in the sun. That I'd watched her step into a world built to free her from fear and thought, *Let me be the one who holds that door.*

Instead, I said nothing. The magic in Middletown was thin; even a whispered truth could tear a seam. And somewhere under the sugar-sticky scent of the bar, something else carried on the air—a sharper scent, metallic and wrong. Watching. Waiting.

She sank a jackpot and whooped, triumphant. The sound arrowed straight through my restraint.

"Not bad," I said, meaning perfect.

She turned to face me fully, heat still in her cheeks, eyes bright. "So, what now? You gonna ask for my number or vanish like most guys who realize they've met their match?"

"I'm not like most guys." A vow, not a line.

For a heartbeat, her gaze searched mine like she

could peel the glamour back with her eyes alone. Then she rattled off her number. I repeated it once aloud for show and tucked it away where nothing could prise it loose.

As I keyed it into my phone, the heart-mark at her wrist flashed—so faint no human would have noticed. The resonance skimmed across my skin, familiar as tide-pull. SoulSync. Valarie had touched her path. My jaw eased. Good. If the world was going to meddle, at least it had chosen a weapon I trusted.

"Until next time," I said, stepping back before I forgot how to. Before I did something reckless, like tell her who I was. What I was.

She held my gaze, smiling like a challenge. "Yeah. Until next time."

I let the night swallow me. The door's hydraulic hiss became a gasp of cool air. Outside, the street-lights cast halos on wet pavement, and my borrowed face wavered—just for a second. A shadow too long for the man I wore stretched ahead of me; a salt-deep thrum rolled under my ribs, the ocean answering something it recognized.

I clenched my hands until the glamour sealed tight again.

Not yet.

Behind me, laughter rose and fell. Ahead, the

wind shifted, carrying that wrong-metal tang again. Old power, jealous and hungry, skirting the edges of town like a shark that knew the taste of blood.

Let it circle.

I had her number. I had her name. And I had no intention of letting fate do all the work this time.

"Next time," I told the dark, and it listened. "I won't vanish."

CHAPTER 3
CLARK

As I watched the stranger disappear into the night, a gnawing ache twisted deep in my chest. The glow of Middletown's neon signs painted his retreating form in shifting blues and pinks, his silhouette briefly swallowed by the dark alley beyond the arcade.

I hadn't even gotten his name.

That realization hit harder than it should have. One moment he'd been at my side, bantering over pinball and drinks, the next he'd melted into the shadows as if he'd never been there at all.

My wrist burned.

I froze, glancing down to see the faint outline of the heart-shaped mark on my skin glowing softly beneath the surface, pulsing in time with my racing heartbeat. A subtle hum reverberated up my arm, sending shivers through my body.

"No freaking way," I whispered, brushing my thumb over the mark. The glow brightened for a heartbeat, then dimmed again like it was teasing me.

This only meant one thing—the SoulSync implant was reacting.

But that couldn't be right. Sabrina had explained this mark only flared when you encountered a soulmate, a Heartbound connection. The idea that a random guy in a bar could set it off was absurd.

Except… he hadn't felt random.

Images from the Arcane Room slammed into me like a wave:

Kade's golden skin gleaming under the impossible sun.

The press of his lips against mine.

The roller coaster ride that had left me shaking and breathless in more ways than one.

The freedom of being seen, wanted, worshipped.

I clutched my wrist, trying to steady my breathing. Could it be him? Could the stranger from the bar somehow be tied to that night, that dream?

I needed answers, and there was only one place I could get them.

. . .

THE STREETS OF CORAL COVE WERE QUIET AS I LEFT Middletown behind, the ocean breeze carrying a briny tang that clung to my lips. A faint mist hung in the air, curling around the lampposts like tendrils of magic. Somewhere in the distance, a seagull cried, its call eerily lonely against the soft crash of waves.

Coral Cove always felt different at night. The human world slumbered while the other realms stirred, their presence slipping through the cracks. Some nights, I swore I saw shadows moving where there shouldn't be any, or caught the gleam of eyes that vanished when I blinked.

Tonight, though, the world felt... charged.

The further I walked toward Coastal Cupid, the more that energy intensified, prickling over my skin. It was like the whole town was holding its breath.

The little bell above the Coastal Cupid door jingled as I pushed it open, and I was instantly enveloped by warmth. The interior glowed with shades of rose and lavender, soft lighting casting playful shadows over heart-shaped decorations and shelves of enchanted trinkets. It smelled faintly of vanilla and cinnamon, like the sweetest parts of a dream.

Sabrina was perched behind the front desk, typing furiously on a floating holographic keyboard. Her head snapped up, and her face lit with pure sunshine.

"Clark!" she squealed, bouncing to her feet. "Perfect timing! You're back sooner than I expected. Do you want to check your SoulSync results?"

Normally, her boundless enthusiasm would have made me laugh, but tonight my nerves were too raw. I held up my glowing wrist. "Sabrina... is this normal? It's been itchy for a while, but now it's... doing this."

The heart symbol shimmered like molten gold beneath my skin.

Sabrina's bubbly demeanor softened as she ushered me toward the desk. "Totally normal for the first couple of weeks," she assured me. "The implant is still syncing with your bio-signature. But let's take a look at the data."

She typed a rapid sequence of commands. A holographic projection bloomed above the desk, displaying a pulse map of my energy signature. Sabrina's voice faltered as she read the results.

"Uh-oh."

My stomach dropped. "Uh-oh? What uh-oh?"

She turned to me, wide-eyed. "Clark, you've already... interacted with someone tonight."

I blinked. "Interacted? Like… what kind of interacted?"

Sabrina spun the display toward me. "See this spike? That's not a casual handshake or a random flirtation. That's soulmate-level resonance. And it's off the charts."

"No," I said quickly, shaking my head. "I didn't meet anyone tonight except—" My breath caught. "Except some guy at the bar. But that was just… pinball and drinks. There's no way."

Sabrina leaned in. "Describe him."

I swallowed hard. "Short hair, built, kind of mysterious. Sexy in that dangerous, ruin-your-life way."

Her face tightened. "Clark… according to this readout, he's not human."

The words knocked the air out of me. "Not human? Like… fae? Vampire? What does that even mean?"

Before Sabrina could answer, the door swung open behind us with a soft chime.

Valarie Cupid entered the room like the night itself had parted to let her through. She was radiant— long dark hair streaked with iridescent threads that seemed to shimmer with starlight, a fitted pink blazer hugging her curves, and eyes that held galaxies.

Sabrina gasped. "Valarie! You're early."

Valarie smiled, warm and knowing. "I had a feeling I needed to be here." She turned her attention to me, and just like that, my nerves eased. It was like she could see into me, straight past all my defenses.

"You must be Clark," she said softly. "You're here a day ahead of schedule."

I nodded. "I… I needed answers."

"Then let's get you some." She moved beside Sabrina, her presence commanding without being harsh. "Walk me through the results."

Sabrina rattled off the details, her words growing breathless. "Clark's readings are insanely high. She's already found someone who could be a match."

Valarie studied the data, her expression unreadable. After a beat, she looked up at me. "Clark, you're compatible with several potential soulmates, some human, some not. Would you be open to meeting them?"

I hesitated, remembering the heat of that stranger's gaze, the electric pull between us. "I'm… open to it. But what about him? The guy from tonight. Could he be the one?"

Valarie's lips curved. "Very likely. But here's something most people don't realize—you can have more than one soulmate. Fifty or more, easily."

"Fifty?" My voice cracked.

"Yes." Valarie's tone was patient but firm. "The SoulSync doesn't just identify romantic matches. It alerts you to profound, life-altering connections. Lovers, friends, allies. Some relationships are fleeting, others last lifetimes."

I stared at the glowing projection. "And you think my match tonight isn't human?"

Valarie nodded. "Your resonance leans toward shadow and fae realms rather than the human one. Which makes sense, given your condition." Her gaze softened. "Your XP has isolated you from much of the human world. But the night creatures? The shadow beings? They live in darkness too. They understand what it is to exist outside the sun."

Her words hit too close to home. I swallowed hard. "My last relationship ended because... because he couldn't handle it. My condition. It was too much for him."

Valarie reached out, squeezing my hand gently. "That pain shaped you, but it doesn't define you. The right partner will see your darkness and call it beautiful."

My chest tightened. For the first time, I dared to believe she might be right.

"Go," Valarie urged softly. "Trust your instincts

tonight. The darkness isn't something to fear, Clark. It's where you belong—and maybe where someone is waiting for you."

THE NIGHT AIR FELT DIFFERENT AS I LEFT COASTAL Cupid. Electric.

I walked along the waterfront, the wooden planks creaking softly beneath my boots. The ocean lapped at the shore, rhythmic and steady, grounding me even as my thoughts spun.

Two matches in one night. Valarie's words echoed in my mind, tangling with the memory of Kade's sunlit dream world and the stranger's smoldering smile.

I stopped at a late-night pizza stand, grabbing a slice and a sparkling water. The food was just an excuse to keep moving, to keep from drowning in my own confusion.

Halfway down the pier, I felt it—a shift in the air, like the world holding its breath. The fine hairs on my arms stood on end.

And then I *knew*.

He was here.

"Hello, Kade," I said, my voice steady even as my pulse went wild. I didn't need to turn around to know it was him. That energy, that presence—it was unmistakable.

"I thought you didn't live in the human world," I added, finally glancing back.

Kade stepped from the shadows, his form different, but his essence—the unmistakable *him*—the same. The air shifted around him, heavy with that same intoxicating pull I remembered from the Arcane Room. My body recognized him before my mind did, every nerve lighting up in wild recognition.

His grin was slow and dangerous, curling at the edges like smoke. "I couldn't stay away. Not after the Arcane Room."

My heart stuttered violently in my chest. *Gods help me.* I'd imagined this moment so many times, replayed that night over and over until I could almost taste the salt on his skin, hear the crash of waves, feel the sunlight warming me in places I'd never thought possible.

Back then, he'd been the center of it all—the sun, the sea, the dream. The only time in my life where walking in the sun wasn't a death sentence. *He* had been possible, a bright, burning reality I thought would vanish when I woke up.

And yet... here he was.

How was this real? How was he standing in front

of me now, in my world? The Arcane Room was supposed to be nothing more than a temporary escape, a fantasy. So why did it feel like that dream had followed me home?

I held out the pizza box in a half-joking gesture, my voice a little too breathless. "Hungry?"

His eyes glinted with dark amusement, sharp and knowing. "No." His gaze raked over me, slow and deliberate, making my pulse stutter. "I recently ate."

Heat rushed through me at the implication, memories crashing back—the way his mouth had devoured me, the way he'd feasted on every inch of me beneath a sunlit sky that could never exist outside the Arcane Room.

I swallowed hard, my voice dropping lower. "Yes," I said softly, almost to myself. "I remember your appetites very well."

Kade's smirk deepened, predatory and possessive, like a wolf who'd found his prey. In that moment, I couldn't tell which of us was more dangerous—him, with his shadowed hunger, or me, for daring to want him all over again.

I finished my slice in silence, acutely aware of his gaze tracing every line of my body. When he moved behind me, I didn't flinch. I leaned back into him, breath catching.

"Is this okay?" he murmured, his lips brushing my ear.

"Yes," I whispered.

His arms slid around me, pulling me tight against him. The world narrowed to his touch, the scent of salt and shadow, the promise of something dangerous and consuming.

"I haven't been able to stop thinking about you," he said, voice rough.

"Me either." My breath hitched. "About the way you fucked me in public… it was the best sex of my life."

Kade groaned, his erection pressing against me. "You think that was just the Arcane Room?"

I turned my head, meeting his gaze. "Prove me wrong."

He growled low in his throat and claimed my mouth, kissing me like a man starved.

In an instant, his lips were on my neck, his kisses hot and demanding. The pier became our world. Clothes tore. Flesh met flesh. I was lost to him, utterly and completely. There was no one else around, just the two of us in this stolen moment, and I reveled in it. I turned in his arms, wrapping my legs around his waist, my dress hitching up as I pressed against him.

Our lips met in a feverish kiss, tongues tangling as

the heat between us built to an unbearable crescendo. "I need you," I gasped, my voice ragged with want.

He didn't need any more encouragement. In one swift motion, he ripped my underwear off, slipping his fingers inside me, and I was already wet, already ready for him. I moaned, the sound lost in the night air as he lifted me, his cock suddenly out and ready. Without missing a beat, he set me down on his thick, pulsing cock, the fullness of him stretching me in the most delicious way.

I rocked against him, my body moving of its own accord as he kissed my neck, my breasts through the flimsy material of my dress. The pleasure coiled inside me, tighter and tighter, until I knew I was on the edge. "I'm going to come," I warned, and as soon as the words left my lips, the wave crashed over me, a hot, explosive orgasm that left me breathless.

But he wasn't done. Before the last ripples of pleasure had faded, he lifted me off of him, moving me to the pier railing. He bent me over the side, entering me again with a single thrust that sent me spiraling into another round of bliss. Every sensation was heightened, every touch electric as he drove into me, his rhythm relentless.

He reached around, finding the sensitive bundle of nerves at my core, rubbing it in time with his thrusts. I was lost, my world narrowed down to the feel of him inside me, the sound of the ocean, and the distant chattering of people at the nearby bars. And then I was coming again, harder this time, the intensity of it ripping through me as he found his own release. The two of us collapsed against each other in the aftermath, our breathing heavy and ragged as we came down from the high. The cool night air wrapped around us, a stark contrast to the heat that had just consumed us. I could feel his heartbeat against my back, steady and strong, grounding me in the reality of what had just happened.

For a moment, we stayed like that, neither of us willing to break the spell. It was Kade who moved first, his hands trailing gently down my sides before he carefully pulled out of me. I shivered at the loss of contact, my body still humming with the aftershocks of our sex.

He turned me around, his eyes dark and intense as he studied me. There was something almost possessive in the way he looked at me, as if he was committing every detail to memory. Then, with a slow, deliberate motion, he reached down and picked up my torn underwear, bringing it to his nose for a brief, almost reverent sniff before pocketing it.

Kade didn't move right away. His breath mingled

with mine as we clung to each other, our bodies still trembling from release. The world felt suspended, like the pier and the ocean and even time itself had fallen away, leaving only us.

Slowly, he eased me back into his arms, holding me against his chest. His hand stroked lazy circles along my spine, and for a moment, I let myself melt into him completely.

"You have no idea what you've started, Clark," he murmured, his voice rough with more than just desire. There was something dangerous in his tone, something that sent a shiver racing down my spine. "This isn't just a fling, or a dream you'll wake up from. You belong to me now."

My breath caught, but instead of fear, there was a wild, reckless thrill in his words. "And you belong to me," I whispered back, daring him to deny it.

Kade's smile was dark and hungry. "Damn right I do. And this?" His lips brushed my temple, a soft contrast to the roughness of his grip on my hips. "This won't be the last time. I'm not letting you slip through my fingers again."

I wanted to stay wrapped in him forever, to let the night stretch on endlessly. But then I caught sight of the horizon. A thin, silvery light had begun to creep along the edge of the sky, faint but unmistakable.

My heart seized. Sunrise.

"Kade," I breathed, jerking upright. "I have to go."

Confusion flickered across his face, then realization. "The sun."

"Less than an hour," I said, my voice tight. "If I'm not home before it rises…" I didn't need to finish the sentence.

A low growl rumbled in his chest, primal and protective. "I hate letting you go."

"I hate it too." My throat tightened. "But I'll come back. I'll find you."

He cupped my face, tilting it up so I had no choice but to meet his burning gaze. "No, Clark. I'll find you." His thumb brushed across my lower lip, tender and possessive. "This isn't over—not by a long shot."

Reluctantly, I disentangled myself from his arms. The pier felt colder without his warmth, the ocean breeze sharp against my flushed skin.

As I hurried down the pier toward home, I glanced back one last time.

Kade stood at the edge of the shadows, watching me go, his silhouette framed by the fading night. Even from a distance, I could feel the promise in his gaze— the promise that no matter what it took, he would come for me.

My wrist pulsed faintly beneath my skin, echoing the frantic beat of my heart. Two matches in one night. Two soul-deep connections tugging me in opposite directions.

And as the first sliver of sunlight touched the horizon, I knew this was only the beginning.

CHAPTER 4
KADE

I t had been seven nights since I'd fucked Clark on that dock, and every hour since had been a slow, exquisite torture.

Her sounds wouldn't leave me. The broken gasp right before she shattered, the way my name ripped itself out of her throat—those echoes nested under my skin and sang to me in the quiet. I could still taste her salt-sweetness on my tongue, still feel the hard, desperate clutch of her body pulling me deeper, still smell her arousal braided into the ocean wind. The memory didn't fade; it honed itself. It made a hunger out of me.

I'd taken lovers across centuries. I'd worn faces, walked worlds, shifted shapes, and learned to keep my needs neat and contained. Clark ruined that discipline in a single night. Now my cock kept a constant ache like a compass needle—always pointing toward her.

I stalked Coral Cove after dark, letting the night fold me into itself. The day crowd would never understand me. The truth of what I was lived best in shadow. In shadow I was honest.

Her neighborhood breathed softly—porch lights embered low, wind chimes gossiping, the ocean rolling its slow heartbeat in the distance. I stopped outside her house and simply stood there, watching the quiet glow at her bedroom window. The urge to go to her front door like a man and knock like a gentleman scrolled through my mind and dissolved. I wasn't here to pretend. I was here to see.

I shifted.

It was as easy as an exhale—the bones loosening, muscles liquefying, my body narrowing, lightening, arranging itself into something quick and silent. Fur slid across me like spilled ink. When it finished, a black cat crouched where a man had stood, tail curled, ears pricked.

I climbed—claws catching wood, finding seams only night-creatures know—and slipped onto her sill.

There she was.

The bedside lamp made a little sun of its own and

poured gold over her shoulders, her throat, the curve of her cheek. She'd pulled her curls into an unreliable knot that kept tumbling loose; a ribbon of auburn kept falling to her mouth, and each time she blew it away, I felt it in my chest. She moved around the room in those soft, worn-in sweats and a thin cami, all unguarded ease. A mortal woman in her den, surrounded by the ordinary: a stack of folded shirts, a plant stubbornly thriving, a book face-down like it had fallen asleep. And her scent—gods, her scent—warm skin and something that thrummed like magic under it.

On her dresser, a frame caught the lamp and flashed. A photo. Clark with two friends, laughing hard, heads tipped together. An empty space where someone's arm should've been around her waist. No man hovering possessive at her shoulder.

Good.

Another picture, older—her with a man: careful smiles, distance in the eyes. My hackles lifted. I wanted to thumb the stranger's face into a blur.

I watched her a few more breaths—her mouth worrying at a thought, her fingers rubbing absent patterns over her wrist—and then she looked up and saw me.

Surprise first, then something like delight. She

crossed the room and unlatched the window. Night air slipped inside and slid its cool hand along my fur.

"How did you get up here?" she murmured, the fondness in her voice catching me off guard. Her fingers found the top of my head and stroked—slow, gentle. The soundless purr that rattled down my spine was a humiliation I accepted.

Then everything inside her shifted.

Her hand stilled. Her head tilted—not to look, but to listen. She rubbed the inside of her wrist with her thumb. The faint heart-shaped mark the SoulSync left there lifted a ghost-glow under the lamp, as if answering a call I hadn't made out loud.

"Who are you?" she whispered.

My body went very still. Instinct, sharper than any hunger, said not yet.

I slid backward off the sill, dropped to the roof, and melted into the branches of the nearest tree. The shift back to human came with a soft crackle of bone and muscle as I crouched on a thick limb hidden by leaves, angled perfectly to watch her window. I could see everything. My eyes see better than any human's; I was close enough to count the freckles on her shoulders.

She stared out into the dark for a long moment, breath fogging a small circle on the glass, then let the window fall shut. The latch clicked. She didn't draw the curtain.

Good girl.

I pulled my phone from my back pocket and let myself savor the little hesitation before I pressed Call. I wanted to walk through her door and take what I came for. But this—this taut wire between us—I wanted to pluck it and hear it sing.

The line picked up on the second ring. "Hello?" Soft. Cautious. Curious.

"Hey," I said, and let all my intent curl under the word.

A sharp breath. "Kade?"

"How'd you guess?" My mouth curved, though she couldn't see it.

"How did you get my number?" Wary now, and I liked the edge of it. She was smart; she always would be.

"Magic," I said, and let it grin through the phone, "and all."

A beat. Then, because she is who she is, boldness slipped back in like it had only stepped out for a smoke: "What are you wearing?"

Heat hit my blood, clean and fast. "Black jeans," I told her, letting the bass roughen. "Nothing else. And you?"

She looked down at herself. I watched her do it. She was still in sweats.

"A cami," she said, voice gone silkier, "and only panties."

I chuckled low in my chest. "You wouldn't be lying to me now, would you, Clark?"

A pause, then the tiniest tremor of nerves I could hear and see—her hands on the waistband, shoving the sweats down and kicking them aside—"Never."

"That's better," I said, and felt my cock respond like I'd hauled on a leash. "Do you want to play a game?"

"What kind of game?" Her voice thinned and sweetened in equal measure.

"Kade Says." I let her hear the smile. "Like Simon Says, but you'll like this one more."

She pivoted on the ball of her foot—one little spin of excitement she probably didn't know she'd made. "Okay."

I took a breath and let command fill my voice. "Kade says: lie back on your bed. Pussy to the window. I want to see."

She hesitated a heartbeat—long enough for my hunger to flare—then climbed onto the mattress and arranged herself exactly the way I asked. Thighs parted. Panties a thin, damp barrier. Lamp-light honeying her skin.

"You like being watched, don't you?" I asked, and I knew the answer.

"Yes," she whispered. The word was a quake that ran through both of us.

"Good girl." I made it praise and claim in one. "Kade says take your cami off. Slow."

She peeled it up, inch by inch, teasing herself as much as me. When it dropped away, her breasts tightened under the cool air, nipples pebbling. I swallowed a sound.

"Do you need a reward?" I asked, because I like to hear her ask for things.

"Yes, sir." A tremble and a smile braided in the two words. "Please."

"Palms over your body," I breathed. "Neck to ribs. Slow. Tease. No touching where you want most until I say."

She obeyed—hands mapping herself, fingers drawing light circles that avoided and promised—then hovered obediently just above her panties.

"Now pinch your nipples. Both hands," I said, and my voice threatened to break into a growl. "Roll them. Harder. Good."

She gasped and arched, offering me everything without moving an inch.

"Panties off," I said. "But don't stop showing me."

She hooked her thumbs, drew them down, and I watched wetness string and break, watched her shiver when the air kissed her bared heat.

The bark under my hand gave with a soft crack as my fingers dug in.

"Kade says… touch your pussy." I kept my tone level by force. "Circle your clit once. Twice. Good. Now two fingers inside. Slow. I want to watch you stretch around them."

She parted herself, found the slick slide, and slipped in with a broken sigh. The angle, the curl, the way her hips lifted to meet her own hand—she knew her body and wasn't shy about it. I devoured the view, the sounds. My breath fogged the cool leaves.

"Tell me how it feels."

"Full," she whispered, voice shaking. "Hot. It…it feels like you."

The thing I keep caged under my ribs snarled and rolled. Leaves shivered. For a half-second my teeth lengthened, my nails pressed points through skin. I pulled the reins hard and felt everything tuck itself away again with a protesting burn.

"Get a toy," I said, when I trusted my voice. "The thick one. Pretend it's my cock. Slowly."

She reached to the nightstand and pulled out a silicone cock—long, wide enough to make my jaw lock—and she licked it before sliding it between her lips. The obscene sweetness of it nearly broke me.

"That's it," I murmured. "Take me in. Slow at first. Deeper on every thrust."

She pushed the toy inside herself and exhaled like something sacred had slid home. Her hips started a rhythm—careful, then confident—her free hand finding her clit and circling, teasing, stroking. The sounds she made were nothing like the world outside her window: honest, feral, *mine*.

I moved closer along the branch without meaning to, leaves whispering. If I took one more step, I'd be at the glass. If I broke the latch, it would be two strides to her bed. I tasted that future like a copper coin on my tongue and didn't spit it out.

"Look at the window," I said, and she did, eyes blown wide, cheeks flushed. "I'm right here."

Her thighs trembled. The toy moved faster. Wet, rich sounds met the quiet night.

"Good girl," I breathed. "Now—hold it in and grind. Slow... there. Yes. Again."

She made a helpless sound that punched straight

through my control. My hand left a crescent of indentations in the bark. Something in me stood up tall and terrible, then sat back down like I'd pushed it.

"Kade," she panted. "Please—"

"Not yet." I wanted to hear her ask properly. "Say it."

"Please let me come." The most beautiful prayer I've ever heard. "Please."

"Who do you belong to?" I asked, because I enjoy the truth.

"You," she gasped. "I belong to you."

"Then come for me, Clark. Scream my name."

She broke.

It was violent, gorgeous. Her whole body bowed —back arched, hair spilling, mouth open in a cry that tore through the room and out into the night. My name rode it, raw and bright and triumphant. I watched every shudder, every pulse of release, watched slick shine across the toy and her thigh, watched a second aftershock ripple as she whimpered through the tail of it and went liquid on the sheets.

I didn't breathe for a long beat. When I did, it was like coming up from deep water.

I put the phone back to my mouth. "It was beautiful," I told her, and let tenderness loosen my voice, just for her. "Watching you come undone for me."

A shaky inhale ghosted over the line.

"Next time," I promised, dark again, "it'll be my cock and my fingers that make you scream."

A small, wrecked noise. "When?"

"Soon," I said. "Very soon."

I ended the call but didn't move. I watched her soften into the bed—legs heavy, breaths evening out, the afterglow turning her skin to warm light. She reached for the corner of a blanket and tugged it over her hips, half-asleep already, and made a tiny, satisfied sound that no one else in the world would ever get to hear.

I should have left then. Instead, I sat with the ache and the certainty.

I'd come to look. I'd stayed to claim. She didn't know it yet, but something old and irrevocable had hooked itself through both of us on that dock, and tonight I'd only sunk it deeper.

On my way down from the tree, the photo on her dresser flashed again in my mind: Clark with people who loved her. A mortal life strung with mortal joys. I could share that, if she asked. I could stand at her porch in a decent shirt and have pizza in a living room where a plant kept thriving. I could do daytime in the shadows, and the shadows at night. I could do both. I would. For her.

But I am still what I am.

I padded through the dark until the house was a quiet square behind me and the ocean took over the air again. I let my shoulders ease, let the night soak back into my bones. The part of me that wanted to turn around, break the window, and curl around her sleep like a possessive storm finally sat down and behaved. Barely.

"This isn't finished," I told the tide and meant it for her.

Distantly, the horizon held its color—black on black, with the faintest iron-grey seam that meant dawn had begun somewhere far off. Not yet. But coming.

I smiled without softness and let it show my teeth.

This wasn't a game anymore. It was a beginning.

And if there was a war to be waged for the space where her life and mine could meet, I would fight it with teeth and tenderness both—until she fell asleep every night with my name on her lips, and woke every dusk knowing she was mine.

CHAPTER 5
CLARK

E very night since Kade had left me gasping and shaking on that dock, I'd dreamed of him.

His hands.

His mouth.

The way he said my name like a promise and a threat all at once.

Tonight, those dreams weren't enough.

I'd spent the last week pacing my tiny house, trying to convince myself to be rational. Two soulmate pings in a single evening and somehow I was still alone in my tiny house, pacing between the fireplace and the window like a moon-tossed tide. The heart-shaped sigil from my SoulSync kept giving little phantom flutters under the skin—warm one second, cool the next—as if it were tapping out a message I didn't quite speak yet.

Text him, I told myself. Don't text him, I warned back. I tried to work; my spreadsheets stared at me, unimpressed. I tried to read; every sentence rearranged itself into his mouth on mine, his laugh against my throat, the way his voice made the word *baby* sound like a prayer he intended to answer.

I did a circuit of the house—kitchen, living room, office the size of a postage stamp, third room that was basically a glorified closet—and ended at my bedroom window, where the night hung thick and steady. Coral Cove midnight was the only time I ever felt normal. The world dulled to a hush; the sky belonged to me.

Okay, I told the window. *Fine.* I thumbed open my phone.

Clark: Hey, what are you doing?

The typing dots appeared, vanished, returned. My pulse hopped.

Kade: I could be doing you, baby girl.

Heat licked through me, shameless and immediate. I had not been a "baby girl" kind of woman before him. Apparently, I was now.

> Clark: That depends on whether you can bring cheesecake and pizza when you come over.

A beat. Then:

> Kade: I'm going to make you beg for it first. If you're a good girl, I'll feed you something sweet, and then something even sweeter.

My breath stuttered. I could've come from the text alone; I didn't, somehow.

> Clark: Yes.

The message sent. For three trembling heartbeats I considered throwing my phone into the laundry basket, crawling under a blanket, and pretending I'd never—

A knock.

"Oh, gods." I smoothed my hair. Checked my camisole. Considered changing. Didn't. My hands were shaking so hard I nearly fumbled the deadbolt.

He stood on my porch like I'd conjured him:

black T-shirt threaded to muscle, dark jeans sitting indecently well on his hips, that lazy, dangerous grin that had ruined me on a pier. A Waterfront Pizza box balanced on one palm; in the other, a cheesecake wearing a ribbon like it had been born to be unwrapped.

"It's after midnight," I blurted. "Everything's closed."

"Not to me." The corner of his mouth crooked higher. "Hi, Clark."

"Hi," I echoed, because vocabulary had abandoned me.

He stepped in past me with a heat that filled the house. I caught the scent of him—smoke and cardamom and something I could only describe as *night*. He glanced around, unhurried, the way someone inspects a place they plan to know well. That look landed on the wide window in my bedroom doorway and lingered in a way that made my thighs go soft.

"It's good to see you," he said, setting the boxes on my counter. "You're…more beautiful in your own light."

"You're very smooth," I muttered, closing the door and fighting a smile.

"I'm very honest." He turned back to me, and the air between us changed temperature. "Hungry?"

"I thought you were going to make me work for it."

"Oh, I am." He slid his knuckles beneath my jaw, a touch that was barely a touch. "But I want you strong for me."

He guided me to the couch, opened the pizza, and made a plate like he'd been born in my kitchen. When he handed it over, our fingers brushed and my Soul-Sync gave a little *hello, yes, that one.* I tried to ignore it and failed spectacularly.

"You could tell I was starving because my stomach growled?" I teased, to keep from confessing that my hunger had very little to do with food.

He shook his head, studying my face with unnerving tenderness. "Because your color's off."

"That would be…my thing." A half-shrug. "You know. Sun allergy."

"Partly," he said, matter-of-fact. "And partly because I read people in their blood."

The slice hovered half an inch from my mouth. "You what now?"

Those wicked eyes softened. "You remember the Arcane Room. You asked me to bite you."

Heat coiled low even at the memory. "I remember," I said, a little breathless.

"I'm not a vampire," he added, amused. "But I'm a shifter whose magic keys off blood. When I take it, a bond forms. A map. That's how I found you again."

"And here I thought it was Google Maps."

He laughed quietly—god, that sound—and then sobered. "The Arcane Room gets called a dream because it keeps people safe. But some rooms aren't dreams so much as…doors." His gaze held mine. "You walked through one, Clark."

For a second, that sunlit beach flashed behind my eyes—the impossible warmth on my skin, the way he had looked at me like light had never been dangerous, only holy. My throat went tight. "And now you're here," I whispered. "Outside of it."

"Now I'm here." He sank onto the cushion beside me, thigh to thigh, and the world narrowed to the space we made. "And I'm hungry for more than your blood. I want your hours. Your laugh. The way you narrate everything in your head when you think no one's listening."

"I—do not—" I began.

"You do," he murmured, heat and humor winding through the words. "And I want all of it."

I hid a tremor with a bite of pizza. "You barely know me."

His hand followed the seam of my jeans, slow enough to be a question. "I know enough to ask to learn the rest." The touch paused. "May I?"

"Yes," I said, without any idea which part I was consenting to. It turned out to be all of it.

We ate like it counted—because for me, it did. I wasn't precious about carbs when the sun could take whatever days it wanted. He fed me a bite, and I returned the favor, and the whole thing made my pulse trip over itself because this was the sort of ordinary intimacy I never let myself want. After the second slice I leaned back, full and floaty, and he looked absurdly pleased with himself.

"You fed me," I accused softly.

"I'll always feed you." He licked a smudge of sauce from his thumb in a way that was illegal in several states. "And now you'll feed me."

"You said stamina first," I reminded, but it came out as a dare.

"Mm. Dessert before dinner works, too." He stood, offered a hand; I took it.

He walked me to the bedroom like he owned the gravity in the room. At the window, he nodded toward the pulls. "Open them. All the way."

The shades whispered up. Night spilled in, cool and velvet, brushing my bare forearms. I felt seen and safe and high on it.

"Now undress for me," he said, voice even, like a promise he'd keep no matter how long it took. "In the window."

Every nerve ending woke up. I peeled off my tee, then the soft black joggers, a deliberate slowness that made my hands shake. The lingerie set underneath was slinky and inarguably *for him.* His pupils blew wide; I felt it like a hand.

"Did you put that on just for me?" he asked, voice roughening.

"Yes." It was embarrassingly easy to say.

"Good girl," he said, a benediction that struck low and sweet. "Come to the bed."

I lay back, knees toward the glass. He climbed after me with a sinuous grace that didn't belong to a human body, and for the first time I saw it, a subtle ripple under his skin like a shadow passing beneath water; the suggestion of claws that never quite arrived. The sight should have unnerved me. It didn't. It made my hips roll.

"I can be anything you want," he murmured, mouth hovering over the inside of my knee. "That's the bargain of my kind. Tell me."

"I want your mouth," I said, blunt and breathless. "I want your mouth and your hands and your cock. I want—" I swallowed. "I want to be ruined and put back together."

His smile was slow devastation. "Then watch the window, baby. Watch yourself be wanted."

He kissed up my calf, my thigh; he pressed his mouth to the lace and breathed. "You smell like I'm home." His tongue stroked the damp gusset and I almost sobbed. He eased the panties aside and gave one long, deliberate lick from entrance to clit that set every muscle in my body singing.

"Gods," I gasped, eyes falling shut.

"Eyes open," he coaxed, laughing softly against me. "Let me see you watch yourself come apart."

I did. The glass returned a ghost of me—hair wild, lips parted, a woman in a black bra and nothing else, knees open to the night. He spread me with his thumbs and tasted me like he had all the time in the world. His tongue…shifted. There was no other word for it. Silky one second, velvet the next, then textured in a way that made my toes curl and my hips chase him. He read my reactions like sheet music and played what I didn't know to ask for.

"You're so wet," he said against my skin, praise and hunger braided tight. "Such a good girl for me."

My hand caught in his hair. "Kade—"

"Mm?" He glanced up—eyes gone darker—and then slid his tongue inside me. He flexed it as if it had joints, stroking and curling in a way that made me see static. He withdrew, sucked my clit slow and precise, then did both at once, and I made a noise that could've summoned storms.

"I need you," I managed. "I need—inside. Now."

He was naked the next heartbeat, like gravity had stripped him. His body was ridiculous, all shadow-limned muscle and something not-quite-human that lived at the edges, promising more. He lined up, pressed in slow enough to feel every inch catch and give, and I clenched helplessly around him.

"Fuck, look at you," he groaned. "Taking me, so pretty."

He started slow. I begged without shame; he obliged without mercy. He thickened inside me—no other way to describe it—like his body was learning mine and adjusting to ruin me better. He rolled my hips on his length, changed the angle a fraction, and my vision blew white around the edges.

"I'm going to touch your tight little ass," he warned, voice thick. "Yes?"

"Yes," I breathed, more plea than answer.

He wet his finger in his mouth; the sight alone made me quake. The slick press at my backdoor sent a shock up my spine; gentled, paused, pressed again, inch by inch. He didn't force; he coaxed. Every time my breath hitched, he waited, murmuring into my open mouth how good I was, how sweetly I took, how filthy and perfect he found me. When his finger slipped past that tight ring and his cock pushed deep at the same time, I swore I felt the world tilt.

"Good girl," he said, proud and tender. "My perfect girl."

There is a kind of pleasure that is all nerve endings and floodlight—too bright to touch. This was that. He set a rhythm that turned me inside out—hips, hand, mouth at my throat—and the orgasm hit like a breaker. I shook apart around him, sobbing, soundless for a beat and then too much sound, stringing his name into the night air as if it could hold me together.

He rocked me through it, gentled, then built me again. His finger left slowly; his hand slid under my hips, tilting, and he fucked deeper, found that spot again and again until I was clawing at the sheets, beyond shame, beyond language.

"Tell me you're mine," he rasped at my ear, not a command so much as a plea dressed like one.

"I'm yours," I said, wrecked and sure. "Kade, I'm yours."

He groaned like it hurt. "Then take me with you."

The second orgasm burned hotter, faster. It crested like a screaming sunrise behind my ribs and detonated, ripping a cry out of me that must have startled the gulls on the harbor. He followed with a shudder that trembled through him into me, spilling heat that made my body clamp and milk, greedy even in aftermath.

For a long time, there was only breath. He braced over me, forehead to mine, and the night came back in layers — the faraway shush of the ocean, the faint tick of the living room clock, the cool kiss of air on our sweat-slicked skin. I floated. He held me while I did.

When my eyes finally focused, he was watching me like I'd hung a new moon over his water. It was too much. It was exactly right.

"Don't move," he murmured. "Let me take care of you."

He slid out with a tenderness that made my chest ache and padded to the bathroom. The washcloth came back warm; his hands were gentler than any lover had ever been with me. He cleaned me like it mattered. It did. He tucked me under my own blankets like I was precious, kissed my ankle for no reason at all, and went to the kitchen.

"Where are you—oh." I smiled when he returned with the cheesecake, two forks tucked under his fingers. He cut me a bite the size of sin and fed me, slow. The sugar melted on my tongue, decadent and silly and perfect, and I laughed, loose and happy, because this was the kind of softness I hadn't let myself want.

"Good girls get cheesecake," he said, smirking, but his eyes were so soft I had to look away for a second.

"Then I'll be very good," I mumbled around a second bite.

"Mm. We'll test that hypothesis later." He set the plate aside, stretched out beside me, and pulled me into the bracket of his body. His heartbeat was a steady drum against my ear.

We lay like that a while, the kind of quiet where two people breathe in time. The afterglow made me brave.

"Full disclosure," I said, tracing a lazy circle over his sternum. "Valarie Cupid set a date for me. In a few days."

His chest rose under my palm; he was quiet for the length of three heartbeats. "Do you want to go?"

"I…don't know." Honesty tasted clean and terrifying. "Part of me needs to prove to myself this isn't a spell I fell under. That I'm not just…easy to enchant." I sighed. "But also I keep thinking about how you looked at me at the pier. Like I was the only thing you were hungry for. And I—" I swallowed. "I want that to be real."

He tipped my chin up, eyes dark and open. "Clark. You are not easy to enchant. You are impossible to forget." His thumb smoothed my lower lip. "I want you to do what makes you feel safe and certain. If that's meeting someone Valarie chose, I can stand it." A beat. "I won't like it."

A startled laugh choked out of me. "Jealous, are we?"

"Focused," he corrected, dry. Then softer: "And in case it helps the calculus—this won't be the last time. You started something I have no intention of stopping."

Something deep in my chest unclenched. "Good." My throat tightened. "Because I don't want you to."

We kissed—slow and sweet, nothing to prove—and when he finally let me have air again, a pale rim of light had started to ghost the horizon. Habit and fear jolted through me. "Sunrise," I whispered. "It's less than an hour."

His arms tightened automatically, protective instinct a reflex. "Do you need the windows sealed?"

"Yes." I glanced at the clock. "I should sleep soon. The…neurological stuff, if I don't."

He brushed hair off my forehead with reverence. "Then sleep, angel. I'll close the house."

"You're staying?"

"If you want me to." A pause. "If you don't, I'll be on your roof until you wake. Either way, you're not alone."

That did me in. I kissed him again, messy with gratitude. "Stay."

He rose, moved through my little home like a shadow that knew all the corners already—drawing the shades, checking the locks, setting a glass of water by the bed because of course he did. When he slipped back under the covers I rolled into him without thinking, fit my leg over his hip, pressed my face to his throat. His hand curved at the base of my skull, the other low at my back, claiming without trapping.

"Sleep, Clark," he murmured. "I've got you."

My last coherent thought was that he meant it. What was somehow more terrifying is that I might let him.

The SoulSync warmed faintly against my wrist as I drifted—one slow, steady pulse, like a promise answering a promise. And for the first time in a long time, I sank into the kind of sleep that felt like falling into a harbor, cradled by the dark, rocked by a tide that knew my name.

CHAPTER 6
KADE

T he first whisper of sunrise thrummed through my blood long before the sky began to change. It wasn't sight or sound that warned me, but something deeper—primal and instinctual. A vibration beneath my skin. My body knew before my mind did, and every cell in me stirred with the need to move, to shift, to flee before the light exposed what I really was.

But I didn't move.

Not yet.

I stayed tangled around Clark, inhaling the soft, warm scent of her hair as she slept peacefully in my arms. Gods, she smelled like everything I didn't deserve—like honey, clean sheets, and the faint tang of saltwater carried in on the night air. She was curled against me, trusting me completely in a way that made my chest ache and my cock twitch at the same time.

The warning pulse in my blood grew louder, a steady drumbeat urging me to leave. My form threatened to slip, the beginnings of a shift rippling beneath my skin. I clenched my teeth, holding myself together by sheer will. I would not let her wake to find a monster in her bed instead of the man she'd just given herself to so completely.

If she saw me like that—if she saw what I really was—she'd never look at me the same way again.

And Clark deserved more than that.

She stirred softly, murmuring something unintelligible. My arms tightened reflexively, as if by holding her a little closer, I could keep the world at bay. Her face was relaxed in sleep, lips slightly parted, a tiny crease between her brows even in rest. She was beautiful like this, bathed in the deep velvet darkness of night, untouched by the cruelty of the sun.

The sun… My gut twisted at the thought of it touching her fragile, mortal skin.

Her condition—her allergy to the very light that sustained most life—was more dangerous than she ever let on. Even a single sliver of sunlight could burn her, poison her, maybe even kill her. I'd only just found her, only just tasted her. The thought of losing her now was unthinkable.

I couldn't let my carelessness be the thing that hurt her.

Carefully, I eased out from under her, moving as silently as shadow. She murmured again, shifting slightly, but didn't wake. My breath caught as she rolled onto her side, curling into the space where my body had been. Her hand slid across the sheets until it found my pillow. She hugged it to her chest and breathed deeply, like she could still smell me there.

Fuck. That nearly undid me.

I forced myself to focus, crossing the room to check her windows. The blackout screens were down, but a thin line of pale light seeped in along the edge of one. Panic surged through me. I yanked it fully closed and secured it, double-checking each lock until I was certain no light could breach this room.

My hands trembled slightly. For me, sunlight was an inconvenience. For her, it was death.

I ran my fingers through my hair and exhaled slowly. I'd never been this careful with anyone before. Never needed to be. But Clark… she was different. Precious.

I turned back toward her bed and paused, watching her from across the room. Her curls fanned across the pillow, a riot of dark red against pale sheets. One arm was draped carelessly over her waist, the curve of her hip just visible beneath the blanket. She was so damn breakable and yet so fierce.

My fierce, fragile goddess.

Would she ever understand what she meant to me? Would she ever consider leaving this fragile human world behind and stepping into mine—the shadow realm where darkness reigned and mortals were either predators or prey?

I didn't know.

Maybe she'd cling to this life, this small town with its cozy bookstores and safe routines. Maybe she'd never want to see the things I'd seen, the creatures that lurked just beyond the veil.

But gods, I wanted her there with me. Not just as a lover, but as my equal.

The thought of anyone else claiming her, even in this world, made my vision go red. The SoulSync device marked her as mine, but fate was fickle. Coastal Cupid could line up fifty potential matches for her, fifty different creatures with fifty different claims, and none of them would matter.

Because I would *not* share her.

Shaking off the dark possessiveness curling through me, I glanced at the nightstand and spotted a small notepad and pen. I needed to leave her something. If I disappeared without a word, she might think I'd abandoned her.

Sitting on the edge of the bed, I hesitated for a moment, staring at the blank page. There was so much I wanted to say—too much.

I wrote.

Then scratched it out.

Wrote again.

Finally, I let my truth bleed onto the page, stripped bare of pretense.

Clark,

Last night was unforgettable. I can still taste you on my lips, and I don't ever want to stop. You've been under my skin since the moment we met in the Arcane Room, and after last night, you're in my blood, my bones, my fucking soul. I've spent lifetimes searching for something I didn't believe existed, and somehow, impossibly, it's you.

Sleep safe today, little goddess. I'll come back for you when the night returns. When you close your eyes, remember me—and know that when I close mine, all I see is you spread

out beneath me, begging for more.
    Yours,
    Kade

I folded the note carefully and placed it on her pillow, right beside her hand.

Leaning down, I brushed a kiss against her temple, lingering for one stolen heartbeat. "Mine," I whispered, so softly she couldn't possibly hear.

The vibration in my blood had become a roar. The sun was rising fast. I had to move.

It took every ounce of control I had to leave her bed, to leave *her*, but I forced myself to the door. I locked it behind me, then stepped outside into the cool predawn air. The world was hushed, holding its breath, a fragile moment balanced on the edge of light and dark.

The shadows welcomed me like an old friend. I let them swallow me whole, my body shifting as I melted into the darkness. Fur rippled over skin, muscles elongating and reforming. For a few breathless seconds, I wasn't man or beast but something in between, primal and ancient.

When I landed lightly on four paws, I bounded into the trees, vanishing from mortal sight.

Behind me, Clark slept safe and unaware. Ahead of me, the horizon bled pale gold.

The sun would rise soon.

But no matter how far I ran, no matter how deep I sank into the shadows, one truth remained, I would return to her.

Because Clark wasn't just a soulmate.

She was *the* mate.

And I'd burn every realm to ash before I let anything take her from me.

CHAPTER 7
CLARK

I read Kade's note for what felt like the five-thousandth time.

The paper was soft now, worn thin at the edges from where my fingers had traced over it again and again, like maybe if I held it long enough I could hold on to him too.

Each word, every curve of his handwriting, was etched into my memory as deeply as his touch had been imprinted on my skin.

Mine.

That single word replayed in my head like a mantra, a vow, and a warning all at once.

I rubbed absently at the heart-shaped mark on my wrist, the one that always seemed to thrum whenever Kade was near, my thumb circling over it as my thoughts drifted back to him. He consumed me—mind, body, and soul. Even now, I could feel the ghost of his mouth on my skin, hear the rough whisper of his voice calling me *baby girl*, *good girl*, his words winding through me until my body ached for him.

But today, I had a date.

A date with someone that Coastal Cupid had matched me with through their elaborate, magic-backed process.

Valarie was certain this was *the one*—or at least one of my most compatible connections. A true soul-mate match.

And yet, as I stood outside the restaurant, my stomach twisting into knots, I couldn't shake the feeling that I was cheating on Kade.

We hadn't defined what we were. No labels. No promises spoken aloud. Just wild, consuming nights tangled in bedsheets and whispered declarations that felt like truths too dangerous to name.

Still, there was something between us—something undeniable. The connection wasn't just physical. It was raw and electric, a force of nature that had wrapped itself around us both from the moment we met.

He felt it too. I *knew* he did.

So why was I here, walking into a date with someone else?

I sighed heavily, sliding Kade's note back into my bag like it might burn me if I held on any longer. The paper crinkled, fragile and precious, a secret tucked close to my heart.

Then I pushed open the door to Golden Chopsticks and stepped inside.

Valarie had chosen the restaurant, swearing it was the perfect backdrop for a first meeting. The space was dimly lit, soft gold light reflecting off lacquered wood and silk-screen dividers. It smelled of ginger, sesame oil, and something warm and comforting. It was... intimate. Too intimate.

The kind of place where two people might fall in love—or, in my case, where one person might unravel completely.

Valarie had given me strict instructions.

No names.

No pictures.

No backstory.

"Let the SoulSync implant guide you," she'd said, her voice filled with that unwavering confidence she always carried.

I had rolled my eyes at the time, but now, standing

here with my heart pounding, I understood why she'd insisted.

This wasn't just a date. It was supposed to be a test of fate.

May, the owner, spotted me right away and waved me over. "Clark! You made it."

Her warm smile helped ease some of the tension in my chest. "Hey, May. Thanks for staying open late just for this."

"Anything for Valarie," May said with a knowing grin. "Your table's ready. Want me to take you over?"

I nodded, my pulse racing as she led me toward a small booth tucked by the window.

The restaurant was quiet, save for the faint clinking of dishes from the kitchen.

It felt private, secret—like the whole world had narrowed to this single table.

I sank into the seat, rubbing at the heart on my wrist again. The gesture had become almost compulsive lately. Whenever I was nervous—or thinking about Kade—I found myself touching it, as if it could somehow ground me.

And right now, I needed grounding.

Had I eaten before coming here?

I couldn't even remember. My stomach felt like a tangled knot of hunger and nausea.

Golden Chopsticks had opened *just for us* tonight.

Valarie Cupid didn't ask for favors often, but when she did, Coral Cove delivered.

May returned with a glass of wine and a reassuring smile. "Appetizer while you wait?"

"Sure," I said automatically, not even processing the words. My mind wasn't here. It was with Kade.

Everywhere I went lately, Kade was there.

His laugh, his touch, the taste of his mouth still lingering on my tongue.

Was this… cheating?

I bit my lip, anxiety prickling beneath my skin. We hadn't talked about exclusivity, but the thought of him with someone else made my chest ache. And here I was, sitting at a table meant for romance, waiting for someone who wasn't him.

My phone chimed, startling me.

> Kade: What are you doing tonight, baby girl?

My pulse leapt.

The words blurred before my eyes.

He *knew*.

Of course he knew. He always seemed to know.

My fingers hovered over the screen, trembling.

Did I tell him the truth—that I was on a blind date arranged by Coastal Cupid?

Or did I lie, hide it, and hope it wouldn't matter?

Neither option felt safe.

Finally, I typed something vague.

> Clark: Meeting someone, but maybe you'd want to come over later?

It was honest without being too honest. My thumb hesitated over the send button.

Then I hit it and exhaled sharply.

The reply came almost instantly.

> Kade: Who are you meeting?

Shit.

I hadn't thought that far ahead.

> Clark: No one important. I'll tell you about it tonight if you want to come over. If not, no pressure.

I tried to make it sound casual, but my stomach was in free fall.

Would he believe me?

Would he show up anyway?

The screen stayed silent. No reply.

My chest tightened painfully. Had I just ruined everything?

Just as I was about to grab my bag and run out of the restaurant, the door swung open.

I looked up—and froze.

It was him.

The guy from the bar. The one who'd played pinball with me, flirted shamelessly, taken my number… and then ghosted me completely.

My jaw dropped as he sauntered toward me, confidence radiating off him in waves. He leaned down before sitting, brushing a kiss against my cheek like we were old lovers.

"It's lovely to see you again," he said smoothly. His scent—warm, dark, familiar—wrapped around me like smoke.

My wrist tingled sharply. The SoulSync chime echoed faintly in my head, unmistakable.

Oh, shit.

I scrambled to cover my reaction. "I'm sorry, did you lose my number? Or do you ghost all your potential soulmates?"

A smile tugged at his lips, amused by my snark. "Only the ones who beat me at pinball."

Deflection. Typical.

I crossed my arms and leaned back. "Okay, so you know my name. Care to share yours?"

Before he could answer, May appeared with a notepad. "Ready to order?"

Grateful for the interruption, I glanced at the menu. "Cashew chicken and an order of egg rolls, please."

May turned to him expectantly.

"I'll have a bottle of O-negative," he said casually.

My head snapped up. *Excuse me?*

May just nodded like he'd ordered a side of dumplings.

Coral Cove was full of magical beings, but watching May treat blood like wine still sent a chill down my spine.

When she left, I turned back to him, my mouth dry. "You didn't answer my question."

"You didn't answer mine," he said smoothly.

"What question?" I shot back.

"Why you're here," he said, leaning forward. "When your heart already belongs to someone else."

My pulse stumbled. He couldn't possibly mean Kade.

Could he?

My eyes narrowed. "Are you reading my

thoughts? Because if you are, get the hell out of my head."

He laughed softly, shaking his head. "I don't need to read your mind to know you're attached."

"Then how?" I demanded.

His gaze sharpened, dark and hungry. "Because I've tasted you before. I know your blood."

The words hit me like a blow. My stomach dropped, breath catching in my throat.

And then… realization slammed into me.

No.

No way.

"You—" My voice faltered. "You're the same person. At the bar. That was *you*?"

He nodded, and in that instant, the entire world shifted. "I told you, baby girl. I'm a shape-shifter. I can be anyone you need me to be."

Before my eyes, his features shimmered, shifting like liquid shadow. The stranger's face melted away… and there he was.

Kade.

My Kade.

I stared, my mind reeling. "Holy shit."

May returned, placing my food and a glass of dark red liquid in front of him. He downed it in one slow, deliberate sip, his gaze never leaving mine.

When he set the glass down, his mouth curved into a wicked smile. "Now you understand."

"You… you tricked me," I breathed.

"I *tested* you," he corrected gently, sliding into the booth beside me. His body heat seared my skin through the thin fabric of my dress. "I needed to know if you'd choose me. Even without knowing it was me."

Tears welled in my eyes. "I didn't want to go on this date," I blurted, the words tumbling out. "But I'd paid so much for the implant, and Valarie set it up, and I just… I didn't want to let her down. I thought maybe—"

Kade reached out, brushing his thumb across my cheek, silencing me.

"I know, baby girl." His voice was velvet and danger all at once. "I knew from the moment we met that you were mine. The SoulSync warmed when we touched, didn't it?"

I swallowed hard. "Yes."

"My implant did the same." His gaze darkened, possessive. "That night in the Arcane Room, when you begged for my touch… there was no going back."

A shiver ran down my spine.

"Kade," I whispered, everything inside me unraveling. "Take me home."

His mouth curved into a slow, dangerous smile. "Gladly. But first…"

He leaned closer, lips brushing my ear. "Let's make the whole town see what it looks like when fate claims someone."

My pulse thundered.

And just like that, I knew this wasn't just a date gone wrong. It was the beginning of something wild, dark, and utterly ours.

EPILOGUE

CLARK

1 Year Later

I woke as the first threads of twilight bled across the horizon, darkness descending like a velvet curtain.

The night always came gently here, slow and soft, wrapping around our little home like a protective shroud.

I stretched, luxuriating in the cool sheets brushing

against my bare skin, my body deliciously sore from the night before. My hand slid across the bed, searching instinctively for him—*for Kade*.

Warmth met my fingertips, and I smiled before my eyes even opened.

He was here.

Always here.

Rolling onto my side, I spooned myself around his body, pressing my face against the broad expanse of his back. I inhaled deeply, breathing him in. His scent was everything—dark spice and salt air, laced with the metallic tang of magic and the sweetness that was purely him.

"Good evening, baby," he murmured sleepily, his voice rough and velvet-soft all at once. The sound of it sent a shiver straight down my spine.

He turned in my arms, pulling me close so that our bodies fit together perfectly, like two puzzle pieces clicking into place. The moment our skin touched, it felt like coming home.

My fingers wandered over him, tracing the firm lines of his thighs, skimming over ridges of muscle and smooth patches of skin. I loved exploring him like this, mapping him out night after night.

He tensed beneath my touch, his breath catching, and a slow, wicked smile curved my lips.

"What do you need, baby?" he asked, voice dropping to that low, commanding purr that never failed to melt me. "All you have to do is be a good girl and *ask*."

Gods help me, he knew exactly what that tone did to me.

I hesitated, my breath hitching.

Tonight, I wanted something different. Something I hadn't dared to ask for since long before I met him.

Finally, I whispered, my voice trembling with vulnerability and desire, "I want you to be a woman tonight. Someone with thick thighs... soft curves... someone I can worship."

His gaze softened, heat sparking like liquid fire in his blue eyes. For a heartbeat, neither of us moved. Then his mouth descended on mine.

The kiss was deep and claiming, his tongue sliding against mine in a slow, deliberate dance that made my whole body ache.

When he pulled back, his smile was pure promise.

"I'll be anything you want, baby," he said, and I knew he meant it.

We kissed again, more urgently this time, mouths hungry, hands roaming. His lips trailed fire down my throat, across my collarbone, before he claimed my breasts with teasing licks and gentle bites. My back arched, helpless under his worship, as he explored every inch of me like I was a sacred offering.

When he reached my thighs, he paused, looking up at me with eyes gone dark and feral.

"Mine," he growled softly. Then his teeth sank into the tender flesh of my inner thigh.

A sharp, intoxicating pain blossomed into pleasure, stealing my breath. I moaned, fisting the sheets as his tongue soothed the bite, licking away the sting.

And then—before my eyes—he *changed*.

It was seamless, breathtaking.

The strong, angular lines of his body softened, reshaping into lush curves and supple flesh.

His broad shoulders narrowed, his chest swelling into full, perfect breasts. His waist cinched, hips flaring, thighs thick and powerful.

When the transformation stilled, a woman lay between my legs. *My woman.*

She had Kade's same wild curls and piercing blue eyes, but her new form was all soft belly, plush curves, and decadent promise.

My breath caught. My desire spiked so sharply it almost hurt.

"Kade," I whispered, awe and hunger tangled in my voice.

She smiled—slow, sensual, devastating. "I know exactly what you need, baby."

Then her head dipped, and her mouth found my aching center.

The first flick of her tongue sent me reeling, pleasure detonating like fireworks behind my eyes. She licked and sucked with expert precision, her shapeshifter's body attuned perfectly to mine. Each moan she coaxed from me felt like a secret being pulled from my soul.

I couldn't just take, though. Not tonight.

I sat up, pushing her gently onto her back, needing to explore this new form she'd given me. My hands roamed over her, cupping her breasts, savoring their weight before taking one into my mouth. She gasped, her back arching, and I smiled against her skin.

"Good girl," I murmured, my voice dark with want. "You like that, don't you?"

"Yes," she panted, her voice breathless and feminine now.

I slid my hand down between her thighs, groaning when I found her wet and ready for me.

"I love how hot you get for me," I said, nipping at her lower lip before plunging my fingers deep inside her.

Her moan was wild, unrestrained, and it spurred

me on. I thrust my fingers in a steady rhythm, my thumb circling her clit until she was writhing beneath me, begging for release.

But before she came, she rolled us suddenly, pinning me beneath her soft, curvy body.

"My turn," she growled, her voice dripping with promise.

I gasped, the world tilting as she slid down my body, spreading my legs wide.

"I'm going to make you scream so loud," she whispered, her breath ghosting over my wetness, "the neighbors will *have* to check on you."

Then her mouth was on me, and there was no thinking, no speaking—only feeling.

She devoured me, her tongue everywhere at once, relentless and skilled. Her hands gripped my thighs, holding me open as she licked and sucked me into oblivion.

My orgasm hit hard, violent and consuming.

I screamed, just like she promised, my voice raw as I shattered apart under her touch.

She didn't stop until I was trembling and spent, the world fading to white around the edges.

When it was finally over, she crawled back up and gathered me against her, wrapping me in the soft strength of her new form.

"I've got you," she murmured, pressing a kiss to my temple.

My breath steadied as I melted into her embrace.

In that quiet, sacred moment, I understood something deep in my bones:

I would never want for anything again.

Kade wasn't just my soulmate—she was *every* soulmate, every possibility, every form my heart might crave.

She was my shadow and my light, my safe place and my wildest fantasy.

As I drifted toward sleep, sated and cherished, the last thing I felt was her heartbeat against mine.

And I knew, with absolute certainty, that I had found my forever in the darkness.

IF YOU ENJOYED *HEARTBOUND SOULS* YOU'LL WANT TO read about the first time Kade and Clark met in the Tarot Fantasies series:

ACE OF WANDS

In the Arcane Room, anything is possible
    —even the sun.
Clark:

I've lived my life in the shadows, never knowing the sun's warmth. But in the Arcane Room, I'm free to dream, to love, and to embrace the possibilities I've always been denied.

Clark's life has been defined by darkness—literally. Her rare condition (XP) keeps her hidden from the sun, but in the Arcane Room, all the rules change. For the first time, she feels the sun's warmth, and with it, a stirring desire she's never known. Enter Kade, a mysterious figure who ignites her passions and opens her eyes to a world of possibilities. As Clark navigates this dreamlike reality, she must decide if the life she's always known is enough—or if she's ready to step into the light of her wildest dreams.

Sign up for Jax Wilder's newsletter and receive a collection of unpublished Coral Cove short stories. Meet familiar characters and dive deeper into the love and romance that Coral Cove is known for. Don't miss out on this exclusive content!

https://mailchi.mp/158597581671/jax-wilder

Jax Wilder

ALSO BY JAX WILDER

CORAL COVE SERIES

Coral Cove Series

Sleighed by Love

Harvesting Love

Dawning Desire

Knead You Now

Love Rewound

Perfect Lover Spell

Haunted by Her

Tarot Fantasies Series

The Devil's Temptations

Strength of the Beast

Hanged Passions

Six of Cups

Death's Embrace

Queen of Pentacles

Seven of Pentacles

Ace of Wands

Three of Swords

Two of Swords

Lovers In The Veil

Stand Alone Titles

Pride and Prejudice and Witches

MIRANDA LEVI

From A Youth A Fountain Did Flow

The Sea Withdrew

A Tear In Time

Mo(ther) Na(ture)

In Orion's Hands

Jackson Anhalt

From The 911 Files

LORELAI HAMILTON

Encyclopedia of Divination

Encyclopedia of Cryptids

Encyclopedia of Faeries

Tarot Tales and Magic Spells

Teenage Tarot

Arcane In Verse

The Eclectic Witch's Grimoire

Teenage Witch's Grimoire

Find Your Bliss

Tarot Reflection Journal

Tarot Refection Journal Coloring The Tarot

Dream Journal

ISLA WATTS: A FAIRY BAD DAY

A Fairy Bad Day

Surprise! You're a Vampire

Gorgeous, Gorgeous, Gorgons

Mork The Handsome Orc

Adopted By Werewolves

Bite Me If You Can

That's The Spirit!

ROSE DAWSON'S BOOK JOURNALS:

My Time With The Fairies

Enchanted Escapades

Enchanted Escapades

Dewey Decimal Diaries

Siren's Songbook

Pride and Prejudice

Bibliophile's Bounty

Book of Books Journal

Pages & Passages Reading Journal

Bookworm's Companion Reading Journal & Tracker

ABOUT THE AUTHOR

Jax Wilder is a passionate romance author hailing from a charming small town nestled in the picturesque Pacific Northwest. With a heart full of love and an unyielding belief in the power of happily ever afters, Jax weaves enchanting tales of love and connection that leave readers captivated.

Jax's novels are a reflection of her commitment to celebrating the magic of love, and her characters' journeys mirror the warmth and happiness she has found in her own life. Join her on the enchanting journey of love, passion, and enduring connection through her heartfelt romance novels.